The Nexus of Deceit

The Nexus of Deceit

UNRAVELING A GLOBAL CONSPIRACY

Anurag Anurag

Anurag Anurag

Contents

1

Code Red

The phone rang with an urgency that cut through the stillness of the office. Startled, Alex Castellanos, the technology genius behind the government's latest venture, glanced at the caller ID before answering. The voice on the other end was unmistakable—the FBI Director himself.

"We are in big trouble. Come soon," the Director's voice crackled over the line before the connection abruptly ended.

Heart racing, Alex wasted no time. Grabbing his jacket and keys, he dashed out of his office and into the bustling streets of Washington, D.C. The gravity of the Director's call hung heavy in the air as he navigated the rush-hour traffic, the weight of uncertainty pressing down on him with each passing second. Horns blared, and pedestrians moved in a chaotic dance around him, but Alex's focus was unwavering.

As Alex raced toward the FBI headquarters, his mind flashed back to the inception of the software project—a project born out of necessity, driven by the government's unwavering commitment to national security. It had started innocently enough, a few years back, with a team of brilliant minds pooling their expertise to develop a groundbreaking system that could revolutionize law enforcement.

The idea was simple yet ambitious: to create a software program capable of using individuals' DNA to track their movements in real-time. The initial focus was on addressing the challenges posed by illegal immigration, with the goal of enhancing border security and ensuring compliance with court appearances and deportation orders. The team envisioned a future where the program could help locate missing persons, track criminals, and even prevent terrorist activities.

Under the guise of protecting the nation's borders, the project gained momentum, drawing funding and resources from government agencies eager to harness its potential. Alex and his team worked tirelessly, refining the algorithms, fine-tuning the protocols, and testing the system's capabilities in controlled environments. Each successful trial brought a sense of accomplishment and pride.

But as the project progressed, so too did the stakes. What began as a noble endeavor to safeguard the country's interests soon took on a darker hue, as concerns arose about the potential for abuse and overreach. Whispers of privacy violations and ethical quandaries circulated behind closed doors, but the allure of technological supremacy proved too tempting to resist. The power to monitor and control could easily be turned against innocent citizens, and the thin line between security and surveillance became increasingly blurred.

Now, as Alex sped through the streets, he couldn't shake the sinking feeling that something had gone terribly wrong. The Director's cryptic message hung in the air like a harbinger of doom, signaling a reckoning that threatened to unravel everything they had worked so hard to build. The traffic lights seemed to conspire against him, turning red just as he approached. Each delay heightened his anxiety.

With each passing mile, the weight of responsibility bore down on Alex's shoulders. The fate of the nation—and perhaps the world—hung in the balance, and it was up to him to set things right before it was too late. Memories of late-night coding sessions and intense strategy meetings flooded his mind. He thought of his team, their dedication, and the trust they had placed in him.

As he neared his destination, Alex steeled himself for the challenges that lay ahead. The imposing structure of the FBI headquarters loomed into view, a stark reminder of the gravity of the situation. Whatever awaited him inside, he knew one thing for certain: the time for reckoning had come, and there was no turning back. He took a deep breath, adjusted his grip on the steering wheel, and prepared to face the unknown.

2

The Race Against Time

As Alex entered the FBI office, he noted the palpable tension in the air. The Director, already engrossed in discussion with his team, glanced up and motioned for Alex to join them. With a sense of urgency, Alex made his way to the table, greeted by familiar faces he had worked along-side during the development of the DNA tracking software.

"Alex, good of you to come," the Director greeted, his voice grave. "We're facing a critical situation."

Alex nodded, taking a seat and absorbing the gravity of the situation. "What's happened?" he inquired, his tone echoing the concern in the room.

The Director wasted no time in briefing Alex on the recent developments. "We've had two suspicious deaths linked to the hacked system," he explained. "One in Paris and another in San Francisco. Both victims were high-profile individuals whose DNA was used to track their locations."

Alex's curiosity peaked as he leaned forward, his expression grave. "Who are they?" he inquired, his voice tinged with concern.

The Director hesitated for a moment before responding, his tone somber. "The first victim was Jean-Luc Laurent, a prominent businessman based in Paris. The second was Marcus Thompson, a rising politician in San Francisco."

A chill ran down Alex's spine as he absorbed the information. These weren't just random targets – they were influential figures with connections that reached far and wide. The gravity of the situation weighed heavily on him as he realized the magnitude of what they were up against.

"So, someone's exploiting the system to target these individuals," Alex mused, a sense of urgency creeping into his voice.

"That's right," the Director confirmed. "We need to act swiftly to contain the situation before more lives are lost."

As the Director outlined the plan of action, Alex listened intently, his mind already racing with potential solutions. "I'll assess the system and see if I can block the hacker's access," he offered, determination shining in his eyes. "Meanwhile, the team can start investigating the connection between these deaths."

With a nod of agreement, the Director turned to address the rest of the team, assigning tasks and delegating responsibilities. Each member of the team responded with a sense of purpose, fully aware of the gravity of the situation at hand.

Outside the office, the city buzzed with activity, oblivious to the impending threat that loomed overhead. But inside the FBI headquarters, the atmosphere crackled with intensity as the team mobilized to confront the unseen adversary lurking in the shadows.

As Alex immersed himself in the task of analyzing the system, he found himself engrossed in a whirlwind of code and data, his fingers flying across the keyboard with precision. Lines of code scrolled across the screen, each one a potential clue in the hunt for the elusive hacker.

"Have you found anything yet, Alex?" a colleague queried, peering over his shoulder with keen interest.

Alex nodded, his eyes fixed on the screen as he scanned the code for anomalies. "I'm close," he replied, his voice tinged with anticipation. "Just need to cross-reference a few more data points."

Across the room, another member of the team approached, a stack of printouts in hand. "I've compiled a list of recent network activity," she announced, placing the papers on Alex's desk. "It might help narrow down the search."

"Thanks," Alex acknowledged, quickly scanning the documents for any relevant information. "Let's see if we can pinpoint the source of the breach."

As Alex worked through the intricacies of the system, his colleague Sarah leaned in, her brow furrowed with concern. "Any luck finding the source of the breach?"

Alex sighed, running a hand through his hair. "Not yet. It's like trying to find a needle in a haystack."

Sarah nodded sympathetically. "Well, we've got to keep at it. Lives are at stake."

Across the room, another colleague chimed in. "What if we're looking at this from the wrong angle? Maybe the hacker isn't after the individuals themselves, but something they represent."

Alex raised an eyebrow, intrigued. "Go on."

The colleague leaned forward, excitement in his eyes. "Think about it. These victims were both prominent figures in the climate change movement. Maybe the hacker's targeting them to send a message."

Sarah nodded thoughtfully. "It's definitely a possibility. We should look into any connections they had, anyone who might have a grudge against them."

Alex tapped his chin, deep in thought. "Alright, let's start digging. We might just be onto something."

"Have we checked the database for any unusual access logs?" one team member suggested, prompting a flurry of activity as Alex and his colleagues delved into the archives.

"I found a discrepancy in the encryption protocol," another colleague announced, drawing Alex's attention to a potential vulnerability in the system.

As they huddled around the table strewn with files and evidence, Agent Ramirez flipped through a stack of documents, his brow furrowed in concentration. "I've found something here," he announced, holding up a sheet of paper for the team to see. "Financial records from the politician's campaign. There's a discrepancy in the funding sources."

Agent Chen leaned in, her eyes scanning the numbers. "You're right. Large sums of money with no clear origins. This could be our lead."

David nodded, his mind racing with possibilities. "If the hacker's targeting individuals who challenge the status quo, these irregularities could be the motive."

Suddenly, the room fell silent as Alex's eyes widened with realization. "Wait a minute," he interjected, pointing to a series of transactions on the screen. "These donations coincide with the dates of the victims' deaths. What if they're connected?"

Sarah leaned closer, her interest piqued. "It's possible. If someone wanted to silence these individuals, they might use financial influence to do it."

The team exchanged glances, a sense of urgency coursing through their veins. With renewed determination, they delved deeper into the evidence, each clue bringing them closer to unraveling the mystery behind the deaths and the elusive hacker behind them.

As Sarah's words hung in the air, the team nodded in agreement, recognizing the gravity of her insight. Director Johnson's gaze hardened, his determination palpable as he addressed the room.

"We need to follow the money trail," he declared, his voice commanding attention. "If there's a financial motive behind these deaths, we'll find it."

With renewed focus, the team set to work, combing through financial records, tracing transactions, and scrutinizing every detail for any sign of foul play.

As the team huddled around the cluttered table, their voices rose and fell in a symphony of discussion and debate.

"Have we checked the financial records for any suspicious transactions?" Agent Ramirez queried, tapping away at their laptop as they sifted through data.

Agent Chen nodded, her eyes scanning the screen. "Yes, and I've found some interesting patterns. There are large sums of money flowing from undisclosed sources into the accounts of both victims."

A murmur of intrigue rippled through the room as they absorbed this information.

Agent Brooks leaned forward, his expression thoughtful. "Could these transactions be linked to any known criminal organizations?"

Agent Taylor shook their head. "I've cross-referenced the data with our databases, but so far, there's no direct connection. It's as if the money appeared out of thin air."

Director Johnson listened intently, his brow furrowed in concentration. "Keep digging," he urged. "We need to trace the source of these funds, no matter how elusive."

Meanwhile, across the room, another group of agents huddled around a separate workstation, poring over social media activity.

"Any luck finding a connection between the victims?" Agent Parker asked, scanning the screen for any relevant posts or mentions.

Agent Garcia shook her head, frustration evident in her voice. "Not yet. It's like they were living in separate worlds, with no overlap in their social circles."

Agent Patel's eyes lit up as they spotted something on the screen. "Wait, what about this? Both victims attended the same charity event last year. Could there be a connection there?"

The room fell silent as they considered this possibility, the hum of conversation giving way to contemplative silence.

Director Johnson nodded thoughtfully. "It's a lead worth pursuing. Let's see if we can find anyone who attended that event and might have information about what happened."

Hours passed in a blur as they worked tirelessly, the urgency of their mission driving them forward. The team sifted through mountains of data, cross-referencing every detail, and chasing down every lead. The tension was palpable, but so was their determination.

Alex's eyes were bleary from staring at the screen for so long, but he pressed on. "I've found something," he announced, drawing the team's attention. "There are patterns here, links between the financial transactions and the victims' activities. It's not just about the money; it's about influence and control."

Sarah joined him, examining the data. "You're right. These transactions coincide with key moments in their advocacy work. Someone wanted to silence them."

Director Johnson's eyes narrowed with resolve. "Good work, team. We're getting closer. Keep pushing. We need to find out who is behind this and stop them before they strike again."

As the hours stretched into the night, the team continued their relentless pursuit, driven by the knowledge that the stakes couldn't be higher. The safety of countless lives depended on their success, and failure was not an option.

3

The Ties That Bind

Director Johnson leaned forward, his brow furrowed in concentration as he addressed the room. "Alright, team. We need to find the link between these two victims – the businessman in Paris and the politician in San Francisco."

As the FBI team continued to analyze the evidence, Special Agent David Brooks and Agent Taylor were tasked with conducting field investigations to uncover any potential leads.

Director Johnson summoned Agent David Brooks and Agent Taylor to his office, urgency evident in his tone. "I need you two in Paris, ASAP.

We need to gather more information about Mr. Laurent's connections and activities," he instructed briskly.

Without hesitation, David and Taylor sprang into action, their training kicking in as they gathered their essentials and made a beeline for the airport.

As they settled into their seats on the flight to Paris, the hum of the plane's engines provided a steady backdrop to their conversation.

"So, what's your take on this whole situation?" David asked, adjusting his seatbelt with a thoughtful expression.

Agent Taylor leaned back in her seat, her brow furrowed in contemplation. "It's hard to say at this point. There are a lot of variables to consider. But one thing's for sure – there's more to Mr. Laurent's death than meets the eye."

David nodded in agreement, his gaze fixed on the window as the landscape below began to recede. "Agreed. It feels like we're just scratching the surface of something much bigger."

As the plane soared through the clouds, they fell into a companionable silence, each lost in their own thoughts. The gravity of their mission weighed heavily on them as they hurtled through the sky, bound for a city steeped in history and intrigue.

Their first stop was the businessman's office in Paris, a sleek skyscraper nestled among the city's bustling streets. As they stepped into the elegant foyer of Mr. Laurent's office, the air was thick with anticipation. The receptionist, a poised young woman with an air of sophistication, greeted them with a warm smile, her French accent adding a touch of charm to her words.

"Bonjour, how may I assist you?" she inquired, her voice as smooth as silk.

David flashed his badge, his expression serious yet polite. "We're with the FBI. We need to speak with someone who was acquainted with Mr. Laurent."

The receptionist's smile faltered slightly, a flicker of concern crossing her features. "Of course, Monsieur Laurent's associates are in a meeting at the moment. I can inform them of your presence and see if they're available to speak with you."

David nodded appreciatively. "That would be helpful, thank you."

As they waited, David and Agent Taylor exchanged a glance, their thoughts racing with questions. What connection did Mr. Laurent have to the recent events, and what secrets might his associates hold? The tension in the air was palpable as they prepared to uncover the truth behind the businessman's untimely demise.

Meanwhile, back at FBI headquarters, Agent Ramirez and Agent Chen delved into the politician's background, scouring through financial records and campaign contributions for any hints of foul play. As they sifted through the data, a pattern began to emerge – large sums of money flowing from undisclosed sources, campaign donations with no clear origins.

Their discoveries sent shockwaves through the team, prompting Agent Ramirez to pick up the phone and dial the Director's number. "Director Johnson, we've uncovered something significant," he said, his voice urgent. "It appears that the politician may have been involved in some illicit activities, possibly linked to the businessman's death."

The Director listened intently, his expression grave. "Keep digging,

Agent Ramirez. We need to know the full extent of their involvement," he instructed, his tone firm.

With a nod of determination, Agent Ramirez hung up the phone, his mind already racing with possibilities. The pieces of the puzzle were beginning to fall into place, but there was still much work to be done.

Back in Paris, David and Agent Taylor listened intently as Mr. Laurent's colleagues shared their memories of the man – his dedication to his work, his passion for environmental causes, and his unwavering commitment to making a difference in the world. But beneath the surface, there lingered an undercurrent of suspicion, a sense that not everything was as it seemed. And as David and Agent Taylor probed deeper, they realized that Mr. Laurent's death may have been far from accidental.

David nodded, his mind already racing with possibilities. "Could their shared beliefs be the key?" he mused aloud, his fingers tapping rhythmically on the table.

Agent Taylor chimed in, her voice filled with determination. "It's possible. Perhaps someone saw their alignment with these causes as a threat and targeted them."

"But who would benefit from their deaths?" Agent Ramirez interjected, his brow furrowed in thought. "And why use our own system against us?"

A heavy silence descended as the team pondered the questions, the weight of the investigation pressing down on them like a suffocating blanket. Each member felt the gravity of the situation, the urgency to unravel the mystery looming large in their minds.

As the day wore on, David and Agent Taylor reviewed the notes and recordings from their interviews, piecing together fragments of information that painted a more complex picture of Jean-Luc Laurent. His advocacy for environmental issues had put him at odds with several powerful figures, including industry leaders and political adversaries.

"We need to dig deeper into Laurent's connections," David said, his voice resolute. "There has to be a link we're missing."

Agent Taylor agreed. "Let's focus on his recent activities, any controversial moves he made, or threats he received. Someone out there had a motive strong enough to kill."

Back at the FBI headquarters, Agent Ramirez and Agent Chen were making headway with the financial data. They had traced several transactions to offshore accounts and shell companies, all pointing to a sophisticated network designed to obscure the true source of the funds.

"Look at this," Agent Chen said, highlighting a series of payments. "These transactions align with key dates in Thompson's campaign. Whoever was funding him wanted something in return."

Agent Ramirez nodded. "And if Laurent and Thompson were both involved in the same environmental initiatives, it's possible their deaths are connected through a common enemy."

The team reconvened to share their findings. Director Johnson listened as each member presented their evidence, his expression growing more severe with each revelation.

"We're dealing with a highly organized operation," he concluded. "Someone with significant resources and influence. We need to identify this common thread and act before more lives are lost."

David and Agent Taylor continued their investigation in Paris, meeting with more of Laurent's colleagues and contacts. They uncovered a series of heated confrontations between Laurent and a powerful lobbyist, Philippe Durand, who had been pushing for deregulation in the energy sector.

"Durand has a lot to lose if Laurent's initiatives succeed," one of Laurent's associates mentioned. "They clashed publicly several times, and Laurent wasn't one to back down."

David's eyes narrowed. "We need to speak with Durand. He might be the key to understanding why Laurent was targeted."

Agent Taylor nodded. "Let's set up a meeting. If Durand is involved, we'll get to the bottom of it."

Back in the States, the financial trail was leading to some high-profile names. Agent Ramirez and Agent Chen uncovered links to several prominent figures in the political and corporate worlds, all with vested interests in the policies Laurent and Thompson were advocating against.

"This goes deeper than we thought," Agent Ramirez remarked. "We need to proceed carefully. These people won't go down without a fight."

Director Johnson agreed. "We'll coordinate with international agencies and ensure every lead is followed. This network needs to be dismantled piece by piece."

As David and Agent Taylor prepared for their meeting with Durand, they felt the weight of the investigation pressing down on them. The stakes were high, and the danger was real, but their resolve was unshaken. The truth behind the deaths of Jean-Luc Laurent and Marcus Thompson was within their grasp, and they were determined to see justice served.

4

A Deeper Web of Intrigue

In Paris, David and Agent Taylor sat across from Mr. Laurent's colleagues, their expressions betraying nothing as they listened. The office's opulent decor contrasted sharply with the grim task at hand.

"Mr. Laurent was a visionary," said Sophie Moreau, a senior executive, her voice tinged with admiration. "He was passionate about sustainability and had many powerful friends and enemies."

David leaned forward. "Enemies? Could you elaborate?"

Sophie hesitated, glancing at her colleagues. "There were threats, veiled and direct. Some believed his environmental advocacy threatened their interests. He mentioned once about a powerful lobbyist who warned him to back off."

David exchanged a glance with Agent Taylor. "Do you have any names or specific instances?"

Sophie nodded. "One name that stands out is Philippe Durand, a notorious figure in the oil industry. They had a heated confrontation at a recent conference."

The pieces began to align. David and Agent Taylor thanked Sophie and left, their minds buzzing with new leads.

Back at the FBI headquarters, the team continued their painstaking investigation. Agent Ramirez and Agent Chen were deep in conversation, surrounded by a sea of documents and computer screens.

"We've traced the funds," Ramirez announced, his voice filled with excitement. "They originate from a series of shell companies, all linked to Durand Enterprises."

Chen's eyes widened. "Philippe Durand again. This can't be a co-incidence."

They quickly relayed the information to Director Johnson, who immediately grasped the significance. "We need to dig deeper into Durand's connections and find out who he's working with."

Meanwhile, in San Francisco, Special Agent Brooks was following a different lead. Marcus Thompson's widow, Eliza, had agreed to meet at a quiet café.

"Marcus was passionate about climate change," Eliza began, her voice trembling. "He received threats, but he never took them seriously. The last few weeks before his death, he was anxious, always looking over his shoulder."

Brooks nodded, encouraging her to continue. "Did he mention anyone specific?"

Eliza's eyes filled with tears. "Yes, a man named Victor Blackwell. He warned Marcus that his environmental policies were stepping on too many toes."

Brooks's mind raced. Another name, another piece of the puzzle. He thanked Eliza and promised to find the truth.

Back in Washington, the team gathered for an urgent meeting. Director Johnson addressed them, his tone urgent.

"We've got two names: Philippe Durand and Victor Blackwell. Both are linked to the recent deaths. We need to gather concrete evidence and bring them in for questioning."

Alex, still engrossed in analyzing the software system, looked up. "I've found traces of the hacker's activity. They used sophisticated methods to cover their tracks, but there's a pattern. It's someone with deep knowledge of our system."

Sarah leaned in. "Could it be an inside job?"

Alex's eyes narrowed. "It's possible. We need to vet everyone involved in the project."

The room buzzed with renewed urgency as the team divided their tasks, each person determined to uncover the truth.

In Paris, David and Agent Taylor, armed with their new information, set up a meeting with Philippe Durand. The confrontation was tense, with Durand denying any involvement.

"You think I killed Laurent? Absurd," Durand sneered. "He was a rival, yes, but murder? That's not my style."

David pressed on. "We have evidence linking your companies to suspicious funds. If you're not involved, help us find who is."

Durand's demeanor shifted, realizing the seriousness. "Alright, I'll cooperate. But you need to protect me. Whoever did this won't stop."

In Washington D.C., the investigation took a critical turn when Alex discovered a new lead. "The hacker's trail leads to an external network, but there's a timestamp that matches the logins of one of our own—Agent Jacobs."

The room fell silent. Director Johnson's face hardened. "Bring him in."

Jacobs, when confronted, was visibly shaken. "I swear, I'm innocent. Someone must have used my credentials."

The team was torn, but the evidence was mounting. As they delved deeper, the web of conspiracy became clearer, revealing a network of corruption, power struggles, and a hacker determined to bring the system down.

5

The Hidden Hand

As the tension escalated, the team worked around the clock. Director Johnson called an emergency meeting, his face grave.

"We're up against a sophisticated network," he began. "Jacobs might be innocent, but we need to be sure. Alex, Sarah, I need you to verify every piece of data."

Alex nodded. "I'll need full access to all systems and logs."

Sarah added, "We should also interview Jacobs's contacts. Someone must know something."

Brooks followed up on the lead with Victor Blackwell. The confrontation was intense, with Blackwell initially stonewalling the questions.

"I didn't kill Thompson," Blackwell insisted. "I warned him, yes, but that's it."

Brooks remained calm. "We need your help to find who did. If you're not involved, prove it."

Blackwell hesitated, then agreed to provide information on others who might have had a motive.

David and Agent Taylor continued their investigation into Philippe Durand. Despite his cooperation, they sensed he was holding back.

"We need more leverage," Taylor suggested. "Something that forces him to give us everything."

David agreed. "Let's dig into his financials, his personal life. There's always a weak spot."

The breakthrough came when Alex and Sarah discovered a hidden subroutine in the software, indicating unauthorized access points.

"Someone's been using this backdoor to manipulate the system," Alex explained. "We can trace it, but it will take time."

Director Johnson ordered increased security and surveillance. "We need to catch this hacker before they strike again."

Brooks's investigation into Victor Blackwell unearthed new evidence—a list of payments to an unknown account.

"This could be our lead," Brooks said, sharing the information with the team.

As they pieced together the clues, a clearer picture emerged. The network behind the murders was vast, involving high-ranking officials and powerful corporations.

"We need to move fast," Director Johnson urged. "Coordinate with international agencies, and let's bring them down."

6

The Reckoning

David and Agent Taylor, armed with new evidence, confronted

Philippe Durand once more. This time, Durand's resistance crumbled. The usually unflappable businessman was visibly shaken, beads of sweat dotting his forehead.

"Alright, I'll tell you everything," he confessed, his voice trembling. "But you need to protect me. I've been threatened. If they find out I talked, I'm as good as dead."

David nodded, signaling for Taylor to start recording the confession. "We're listening, Mr. Durand. Start from the beginning."

Durand took a deep breath, then began to unravel the web of deceit and corruption he was entangled in. He spoke of secret meetings, illegal transactions, and powerful figures pulling the strings behind the scenes. The more he revealed, the clearer it became that this conspiracy was much larger than they had initially thought.

Meanwhile, Brooks and his team tracked the payments to a shadowy figure known as "The Broker," a notorious middleman in the criminal underworld. The Broker was a ghost, rarely seen but always felt. His connections ran deep, and he had a reputation for making problems disappear—permanently.

After days of surveillance and careful planning, Brooks and his team zeroed in on The Broker's location. Adrenaline pumped through their veins as they prepared for the raid. "We've got him," Brooks said, a steely determination in his eyes. "Let's bring him in."

The operation was executed with military precision. The team moved in swiftly, catching The Broker off guard. He was apprehended without a fight, his arrogance giving way to fear as he realized the net had closed around him.

Back in Washington, D.C., Alex and Sarah's relentless efforts finally paid off. They had painstakingly traced the hacker's digital footprints, piecing together a complex puzzle of coded messages and encrypted files. The breakthrough came when they discovered a hidden subroutine in the software, indicating unauthorized access points.

"Someone's been using this backdoor to manipulate the system," Alex explained, his voice filled with a mix of excitement and frustration. "We can trace it, but it will take time."

Director Johnson, aware of the stakes, ordered increased security and surveillance. "We need to catch this hacker before they strike again," he commanded, the urgency in his voice spurring the team into action.

The raid was swift and decisive. The hacker, a disgruntled former employee with a vendetta against the system, was apprehended. As the agents led the hacker away in handcuffs, there was a palpable sense of relief among the team. One major threat had been neutralized, but the battle was far from over.

With the hacker in custody, the network began to unravel. Philippe Durand and Victor Blackwell's testimonies led to the arrests of several high-profile individuals involved in the conspiracy. These were not just small-time criminals but influential figures in politics, business, and law enforcement. The revelations sent shockwaves through the corridors of power.

As the dust settled, Director Johnson addressed the team in a solemn yet triumphant tone. "We've faced one of our toughest challenges, but we've come out stronger. Excellent work, everyone."

The room erupted in applause, but it was more than just a celebration —it was a collective sigh of relief. Alex, Sarah, David, Brooks, and the rest of the team shared a moment of triumph, knowing they had thwarted a major threat to national security. The sense of camaraderie and shared purpose was palpable, binding them together in their commitment to justice.

9 798886 922589 4